Goosebumps

Werewolf Skin

Over the harsh gasps of my breath, I listened for the heavy, thudding footsteps behind me. The animal growls.

Was the creature still chasing me?

I grabbed a smooth, damp tree trunk and stopped. I hugged the trunk, struggling to keep my legs from collapsing, struggling to catch my breath.

I turned and gazed back.

Nothing there.

No growls. No grunts. No bang of heavy feet on the ground.

I sucked in breath after breath. My lungs burned. My mouth felt so dry, I couldn't swallow.

I'm okay, I told myself. I'm safe—for now.

I gazed into the deep darkness.

And the creature hit me from behind.

Goosebumps

Werewolf Skin

R. L. Stine

Hippo

Scholastic Children's Books,
Commonwealth House, 1–19 New Oxford Street, London WC1A 1NU, UK
a division of Scholastic Ltd
London ~ New York ~ Toronto ~ Sydney ~ Auckland

First published in the USA by Scholastic Inc., 1997
First published in the UK by Scholastic Ltd, 1998

ISBN 0 590 11344 5

Typeset by Rowland Phototypesetting Ltd, Bury St Edmunds, Suffolk
Printed by Cox & Wyman Ltd, Reading, Berks.

10 9 8 7 6 5 4 3 2 1

I stepped down from the bus and squinted into the sunlight. Shielding my eyes with one hand, I searched the small car park for Uncle Colin and Aunt Marta.

I didn't remember what they looked like. I hadn't seen them since I was four, eight years before.

But the Wolf Creek bus station was so tiny. Just a little wooden shack in the middle of a car park. I knew I couldn't miss them.

"How many suitcases?" the bus driver growled out of the side of his mouth. Despite the cold October air, he had a damp sweat stain on the back of his grey uniform.

"Just one," I said. I was the only passenger to get off at Wolf Creek.

Across from the bus station, I saw a petrol station and a one-block stretch of small shops. Beyond that, I could see the woods. The trees shimmered yellow and brown, the autumn leaves still clinging to their branches. Dry, brown leaves fluttered across the car park.

The driver grunted as he hoisted up the sliding door to the luggage compartment. He pulled out a black bag. "This yours, kid?"

I nodded. "Yeah. Thanks."

I shivered from a gust of cold wind. I wondered if Mum and Dad had packed enough warm clothes for me. They'd had to send me off in such a hurry.

They weren't expecting to be called out of the country on business just before Hallowe'en. They'd had to fly to France. And they'd had to find a place for me to stay for two weeks. Maybe longer.

My aunt and uncle were the lucky winners!

I adjusted the camera bag on my shoulder. I had kept my camera on my lap the whole bus ride. I hadn't wanted it bouncing round in the luggage compartment.

My camera is the most valuable thing I own. I don't go anywhere without it. And I seldom let it out of my sight.

The driver slid my suitcase over the concrete to me. He slammed shut the luggage compartment. Then he started back into the bus. "Someone picking you up?"

"Yes," I replied, searching for Uncle Colin and Aunt Marta again.

A mud-splattered blue van squealed into the

car park. The horn honked. I saw a hand waving to me from the passenger window.

"There they are!" I told the bus driver. But he had already climbed back inside and shut the door. The bus hissed and groaned, and pulled away.

"Alex—hi!" Aunt Marta called from the van.

I picked up my suitcase and trotted over to them. The van screeched to a stop. Uncle Colin climbed out from behind the wheel. Aunt Marta came running from the other side.

I didn't remember them at all. I had pictured them as young and dark-haired. But they were both pretty old-looking. They were both very tall and lean. As they hurried across to me, they reminded me of two skinny grasshoppers with tufts of grey hair on their heads.

Aunt Marta wrapped me in a hug. Her arms felt so bony. "Alex—it's so wonderful to see you! I'm so glad you came!" she exclaimed.

She let go quickly and backed away. "Uh-oh. I'm crushing your camera case!"

I shifted it round my neck. "No, it's a hard case," I replied. "It's okay."

Smiling, Uncle Colin shook hands with me. His wavy grey hair fluttered in the breeze. His cheeks were red and sort of cracked. Age lines, I suppose.

"You're so big and grown-up," he said, "I'm going to have to call you Mr Hunter instead of Alex."

3

I laughed. "No one calls me Mr Hunter—yet," I told him.

"How was the long bus ride?" he asked.

"Bumpy," I told him. "I don't think the driver missed a single pothole! And the man next to me had the hiccups the whole way."

Aunt Marta chuckled. "Sounds like a fun trip."

Uncle Colin lowered his eyes to my camera case. "Like to take pictures, Alex?"

I nodded. "Yes. I want to be a photographer someday. Just like you two."

Their smiles grew wider. That seemed to please them.

But Uncle Colin's smile faded quickly. "It's a hard way to make a living," he said. "Lots of travelling. We never stay in one place for long."

Aunt Marta sighed. "That's why we haven't seen you for so many years." She hugged me again.

"I was hoping I could go out on a shoot with you," I said. "I bet you two could teach me a lot!"

Uncle Colin laughed. "We'll teach you *all* our secrets."

"You're staying for at least two weeks," Aunt Marta added, "so we'll have plenty of time for photography lessons."

"Not if we spend the whole time in this car park!" Uncle Colin declared. With a groan, he hoisted my suitcase into the back of the van.

4

We climbed in. And a few seconds later, we pulled away from the bus station, into town.

A post office whirred past. Then a small grocery and a dry cleaner. We crossed a street, and thick woods surrounded us on both sides.

"Is that all there is?" I cried.

"Alex," Aunt Marta replied, "you've just had the grand tour of Wolf Creek."

"Hope you won't be bored in such a tiny town," Uncle Colin added, turning the van sharply as the road curved through the trees.

"No way!" I cried. "I really want to explore the woods."

I'm a city kid. I seldom even get to *touch* a tree. Going into the woods, I thought, will be so interesting—like visiting another planet.

"I want to shoot a *hundred* rolls of film in the woods!" I declared. The van bumped hard, sending my head bouncing against the van roof.

"Slow down, Colin!" Aunt Marta scolded. She turned back to me. "Your uncle only knows one speed—*light speed*."

"Speaking of light, we'll show you some tricks for shooting outdoors," Uncle Colin said, pressing his foot even harder on the accelerator.

"I've entered a photography competition back at home," I told them. "I want to snap a great Hallowe'en photo. Something really wild to win the competition."

"Oh, that's right. Hallowe'en's only a couple

of days off," Aunt Marta said, glancing at my uncle. She turned back to me. "What do you want to be for Hallowe'en, Alex?"

I didn't have to think about it. I'd already decided at home.

"A werewolf," I told her.

"NO!" she screamed.

Uncle Colin also let out a cry.

The van ploughed through a stop sign. I flew off the seat and hit the door hard. And stared helplessly through the bouncing windscreen—as we swerved into the path of a roaring truck.

"AAAAAIIIII!"

Was that *me* screaming?

Our van rocked violently. I bounced again. Landed on my knees on the floor.

Uncle Colin swerved on to the grassy shoulder.

I saw a blur of red—and heard the truck roar past. Its horn blared angrily.

Uncle Colin slowed to a stop under the trees. His wrinkled face had turned red. He swept both hands back over his thick grey hair.

"Colin, what happened?" Aunt Marta asked softly.

"Sorry," he muttered. He took a deep breath. "Suppose I just wasn't concentrating."

Aunt Marta *tsk-tsk*ed. "Nearly got us killed." She turned in the passenger seat to gaze at me. "Alex—you okay?"

"Yes. I'm fine," I told her. "I didn't expect it to be so exciting here!" I tried to make a joke. But my voice came out a bit shaky.

7

My camera case had fallen to the floor. I picked it up, opened it, and checked the camera. It seemed okay.

Uncle Colin shifted into Drive and pulled the van back on to the road. "Sorry about that," he murmured. "I'll be more careful. Promise."

"You were thinking about the Marlings again—weren't you?" Aunt Marta accused him. "When Alex said *werewolf*, you started thinking about them, and—"

"Be quiet, Marta!" Uncle Colin snapped. "Don't talk about them now. Alex has just arrived. Do you want to scare him before we even get home?"

"Huh? Who are the Marlings?" I demanded, leaning to the front.

"Never mind," Uncle Colin replied sharply. "Sit back."

"They're not important," Aunt Marta said. She turned to the windscreen. "Hey—we're almost home."

The sky seemed to darken. The old trees grew over the narrow road, their leaves blocking the sunlight.

Watching the blur of red and yellow as the woods swept past, I thought hard. My aunt and uncle were certainly acting a little strange, I decided. I wondered why Uncle Colin had snapped at my aunt so angrily when she'd mentioned the Marlings.

"Why do they call it Wolf Creek?" I asked.

"Because the name Chicago was already taken!" Aunt Marta joked.

"There used to be wolves in the woods," Uncle Colin explained softly.

"*Used* to be!" my aunt exclaimed. She lowered her voice to a whisper, but I could still hear her. "Why don't you tell Alex the truth, Colin?"

"Be quiet!" he repeated through clenched teeth. "Why do you want to scare him?"

Aunt Marta turned to the passenger window. We drove on in silence for a while.

The road curved, and a small circle came into view. Three houses stood nearly side by side on the circle. I could see the woods stretching on behind the houses.

"That's our house—in the middle," Uncle Colin announced, pointing.

I gazed out at it. A small, square white house on top of a neat, recently mown front lawn. A long, low, ranch-style house—grey with black shutters—stood to the right.

The house on the left was nearly hidden by overgrown bushes. Tall weeds rose up over the patchy front garden. A broken tree branch lay in the middle of the driveway.

Uncle Colin pulled the van up the driveway to the middle house. "It's small—but we're not here that often," he said.

Aunt Marta sighed. "Always travelling."

9

She turned back to me. "There's a nice girl who lives next door." She pointed to the ranch-style house on the right. "She's twelve. Your age, right?"

I nodded.

"Her name is Hannah. She's very cute. You should make friends with her so you won't be lonely."

Cute?

"Any *boys* in the neighbourhood?" I asked.

"I don't think so," my aunt replied. "Sorry."

My uncle stopped the van at the top of the driveway. We climbed out. I stretched my arms over my head. All my muscles ached. I'd been sitting for over six hours!

I glanced at the grey shingle house on the right. Hannah's house. I wondered if she and I *would* become friends.

Uncle Colin unloaded my suitcase from the back of the van.

I turned to the house on the left. What a wreck! The house was completely dark. Some shutters had fallen off. Part of the front veranda had caved in.

I crossed the driveway and took a few steps closer to the weird, run-down house. "Who lives there?" I asked my aunt.

"Stay away from there, Alex!" Uncle Colin screamed. "Don't ask questions about them! *Just stay away from that house!*"

"Calm down, Colin," Aunt Marta told my uncle. "Alex isn't going over there."

She turned to me. "The Marlings live in that house," she said, lowering her voice to a whisper. She raised a finger to her lips. "No more questions—okay?"

"Just stay away from there," Uncle Colin growled. "Come and help me unload the van."

I took one last glance at the run-down wreck of a house. Then I trotted over to help my uncle.

It didn't take long to unpack. Aunt Marta helped me in the guest room while Uncle Colin made us turkey sandwiches in the kitchen.

My room was small and narrow, about the size of my wardrobe at home. The tiny wardrobe smelled of mothballs. But Aunt Marta said the odour would go away if we left the wardrobe door and the window open.

I crossed the tiny room to open the window. And saw that it faced the Marlings' house next

11

door. A rusted wheelbarrow tilted against the Marlings' side wall. The windows were dark and coated with dust.

I squinted into the window opposite mine—and thought about Uncle Colin's shouted warning.

Why was he so worried about the Marlings?

I raised the window and turned back to my aunt. She tucked the last of my T-shirts into the top dresser drawer. "The room is small. But I think you'll be cosy here, Alex," she said. "And I cleared all the junk off the desktop so you'll have a place to do homework."

"Homework?" I uttered.

Then I remembered. I'd promised to go to the local school for the weeks I stayed in Wolf Creek.

"Hannah will take you to school on Monday morning," Aunt Marta promised. "She is in sixth grade too. She'll show you round."

I didn't want to think about going to a strange school. I picked up my camera. "I can't wait to get into the woods and take some shots," I told my aunt.

"Why don't you go after lunch?" she suggested. Straightening her grey hair, she led the way through the short hall to the kitchen.

"All moved in?" Uncle Colin asked. He was pouring orange juice into three glasses. The sandwiches were set out on the small, round kitchen table.

Before I could answer him, we heard a hard knock on the back door. Aunt Marta opened it, and a girl about my age walked in. Hannah.

Hannah was tall and thin, a few centimetres taller than me. Aunt Marta was right. Hannah was quite cute. She had straight black hair, olive-green eyes and a nice smile. She wore a big green sweater pulled down over black tights.

Aunt Marta introduced us. We both said, "Hi."

I hate meeting new people. It's always so awkward.

Aunt Marta asked Hannah if she'd like a turkey sandwich. "No, thanks," Hannah replied. "I've already had lunch."

I liked her voice. It was really low and husky. A bit hoarse.

"Alex has just arrived on the bus," Aunt Marta told her. "That's why we're having such a late lunch."

I gobbled my sandwich down in a few seconds. I think I hadn't realized how hungry I was.

"Hannah, why don't you and Alex do some exploring in the woods?" Uncle Colin suggested. "He's a city kid. You'll have to show him what a tree is!"

Everyone laughed.

"I've seen lots of them in films!" I joked.

Hannah had a great, husky laugh.

"I want to take a million photos," I told her, grabbing my camera case.

13

"You're into photography?" Hannah asked. "Just like your aunt and uncle?"

I nodded.

"I hope you have colour film," Hannah said. "The autumn leaves are really awesome now."

We said goodbye to Uncle Colin and Aunt Marta and headed out of the front door. A red afternoon sun was sinking behind the trees. It made our shadows stretch long and skinny over the grass.

"Hey—you're stepping on my shadow!" Hannah protested, grinning. She swung her leg to make her shadow kick my shadow.

"Ow!" I cried. I swung my fist, and my shadow slugged her shadow.

We had a good shadow fight, punching and kicking. Finally, she stamped on my shadow with both of her trainers. And I dropped to the ground, making my shadow slump over the grass in a dead faint.

As I sat up, Hannah had her head thrown back, laughing. Her straight black hair blew wildly round her face.

I pulled my camera from the case and quickly snapped a photo of her.

She stopped laughing. And straightened her hair with both hands. "Hey—why did you do that?"

I shrugged. "Just wanted to."

I climbed to my feet and raised the camera

to my eye. I turned and pointed it towards the Marlings' house next door. I took a few steps towards the house, trying to frame it in my view-finder.

"Hey—!" I cried out as Hannah grabbed my arm.

"Alex—don't take a picture!" she warned in a throaty whisper. "They'll *see* you!"

"So what?" I shot back. But I felt a shiver as I saw something move in the dark front window.

Was someone staring out at us?

I lowered my camera.

"Come on, Alex." Hannah tugged me towards the back. "Are we going into the woods or not?"

I squinted up at the Marlings' house. "Why was my uncle so upset when I asked about that house?" I asked Hannah. "What's the big deal?"

"I don't really know," she replied, dropping my arm. "The Marlings are supposed to be a weird old couple. I've never seen them. But . . . I've heard stories about them."

"What kind of stories?" I demanded.

"Frightening stories," she whispered.

"No. Really. What kind of stories?" I insisted.

She didn't answer. Her olive-green eyes narrowed at the broken veranda, the faded, stained shingles. "Let's just stay away from there, Alex."

She started jogging along the side of the house towards the back garden. But I didn't follow her.

15

I crossed the driveway and stepped into the tall weeds of the Marlings' front garden.

"Alex—stop! Where are you going?" Hannah called.

Holding my camera at my waist, I made my way quickly up to the house. "I'm a city kid," I told Hannah. "I don't scare easily."

"Alex, please—" Hannah pleaded. "The Marlings don't like kids. They don't like anyone coming up to their house. Please. Let's go to the woods."

I stepped up carefully on to the rotting floorboards of the front veranda. I raised my eyes to the front window.

The reflection of the setting, red sun filled the glass. For a moment, it appeared that the window was on fire.

I had to look away.

Then, as the sunlight faded from the window-pane, I turned back—and gasped.

Inside the house, the window curtains were slashed and torn.

As if some kind of animal had clawed them, clawed them to shreds.

"Hannah—have you seen this?" I called. I couldn't take my eyes off the shredded curtains.

She stood on the other side of the driveway, leaning her back against my aunt and uncle's house. "I don't want to come over there," she said softly, folding her arms over her chest.

"But the curtains—" I started.

"I told you they're weird," Hannah said sharply. "And they don't like kids gawking through their windows. Come on, Alex."

I backed away from the Marlings' house. My shoe caught on a raised floorboard of the rotting veranda, and I nearly fell.

"Are we going to the woods or not?" Hannah asked impatiently.

"Sorry." I pulled my shoe free and followed her towards the back. "Tell me more about the Marlings," I said, jogging to catch up with her. "Tell me some of the frightening stories you heard about them."

"No way," Hannah replied in her breathy voice.

We trotted across my aunt and uncle's back garden. The tall yellow and red trees of the woods, tilting in afternoon shadows, stretched beyond the smooth lawn.

"Please?" I begged.

"Maybe in a few days, after Hallowe'en," Hannah replied. "After the full moon."

I followed Hannah's gaze to the sky. A bright white moon—almost as round as a tennis ball—rose over the trees, even though it was still daylight.

Hannah shuddered. "I hate it when the full moon comes," she said. "I'll be so happy when it's gone."

"Why?" I demanded. "What's the big deal about a full moon?"

She gazed back at the Marlings' house. And didn't reply.

We made our way through the trees. The fading sunlight filtered through the leaves, sending shimmering spots of gold over the ground. Our shoes crackled over twigs and dead leaves.

I found a gnarled old tree, bent over like an old man. The bark was pitted and wrinkled like aged brown skin. Fat grey roots reached up from the dirt.

"Wow! This is *so cool*!" I declared, pulling my camera from the case.

Hannah laughed. "You really are a city kid."

"But—look at this tree!" I declared. "It's like—it's like it's alive!"

She laughed again. "Trees *are* alive, Alex!"

"You know what I mean," I grumbled.

I started to snap photos of the bent, old tree. I stepped back and leant against a tilted birch tree. I tried to frame the old tree so that its shape looked human.

Then I moved all round the tree, photographing its creases, its wrinkles. I shot one slender branch that lowered itself to the ground like a weary arm.

I dropped down to my knees and snapped the roots reaching up from the ground like skinny legs.

A soft buzz made me raise my gaze. A hummingbird hovered over a flowering weed. I turned and tried to capture the tiny bird in my camera lens.

But the hummingbird was too fast for me. It darted away before I could snap my shutter.

I climbed to my feet. Hannah was sitting cross-legged on the ground, crunching dead leaves between her hands.

"Doesn't that hummingbird know summer is over?" I murmured.

She stared at me blankly, as if she had forgotten I was there. "Oh. Sorry, Alex. I didn't see it." She climbed to her feet.

"What happens if you keep going straight?" I asked, pointing deeper into the woods.

"You come to Wolf Creek," Hannah replied. "I'll show you the creek next time. But we'd better get going. We should get out of the woods before the sun goes down."

I suddenly thought of the wolves Uncle Colin had told me about. The wolves that gave Wolf Creek its name.

"The wolves that used to live here in these woods," I said. "They've all gone—right?"

Hannah nodded. "Yes. They've gone."

And then a shrill howl rose up—so close, so close behind me. The high, shrill wail of a wolf.

And I opened my mouth in a terrified scream.

I stumbled back against the birch tree. My camera banged against the trunk, but I didn't drop it.

"Hannah—?" I choked out. Her eyes were wide with surprise.

But before she could reply, two boys burst out from behind a tall evergreen shrub. They tossed back their heads and howled like wolves.

"Hey—*you* two!" Hannah exclaimed, making a disgusted face.

They were both short and thin, both with straight black hair and dark brown eyes. They finished their howls, then gazed at me, gazed at me hungrily, like wolves.

"Did we scare you?" one of them teased, his dark eyes flashing excitedly. He wore a dark brown sweater pulled down over black denim jeans. He had a long purple wool muffler wrapped round his neck.

21

"You two always scare me!" Hannah joked. "Your *faces* give me nightmares!"

The other boy wore a baggy grey sweatshirt and baggy khakis that dragged on the ground. He threw back his head and let out another shrill wolf howl.

Hannah turned to me. "They're in my class," she explained. "That one is Sean Kiner." She pointed to the boy with the purple muffler. "And he's Arjun Khosla."

"Arjun?" I struggled with the name.

"It's Indian," he explained.

"Hannah told us you were coming," Sean said, grinning.

"You're a city kid, right?" Arjun asked.

"Well, yeah. Cleveland," I murmured.

"So how do you like Wolf Creek?" Arjun asked. It didn't sound like a question. It sounded like a challenge.

They both stared at me with their dark eyes, studying me as if I were some kind of weird fungus.

"I—I've only just got here," I stammered.

They exchanged glances. "There are some things you should know about the woods," Sean said.

"Like what?" I asked.

He pointed to my feet. "Like you shouldn't stand in a big clump of poison ivy!"

"Huh?" I jumped back. And stared at the ground.

They both laughed.

There wasn't any poison ivy.

"You two are about as funny as dog puke," Hannah sneered.

"You ought to know. You eat it for breakfast!" Sean replied.

He and Arjun laughed and slapped each other a high five.

Hannah sighed. "Remind me to laugh later," she muttered, rolling her eyes.

For some reason, that started the two boys howling again.

When they stopped, Sean reached for my camera. "Can I see it?"

"Well . . ." I pulled back. "It's a very expensive camera," I told him. "I really don't like anyone else touching it."

"Ooooh. Expensive!" he teased. "Is it cardboard? Let me see it!" He grabbed for it again.

"Take my picture," Arjun demanded. He pulled his lips apart with two fingers and stuck out his tongue.

"That's an improvement!" Hannah told him.

"Take my picture!" Arjun repeated.

"Give Alex a break," Hannah snapped. "Get out of his face, you two."

Arjun pretended to be hurt. "Why won't he take my picture?"

"Because he doesn't take animal photos!" Hannah sneered.

23

Sean laughed—and snatched the camera from my hands.

"Hey—come on!" I pleaded. I made a grab for it and missed.

Sean threw the camera to Arjun. Arjun raised it and pretended to snap Hannah's photo. "Your face cracked the lens!" he exclaimed.

"I'm going to crack *your* face!" Hannah threatened.

"It's a really expensive camera," I repeated. "If anything happens to it—"

Hannah swiped the camera out of Arjun's hands and handed it back to me.

I cradled it in my arms. "Thanks."

The two boys moved towards me menacingly. Their dark eyes gleamed. Again, watching them approach, their faces so hard, their eyes so cold, I thought of wild animals.

"Leave him alone," Hannah scolded.

"We're just kidding," Arjun replied. "We weren't going to hurt the camera."

"Yeah. We're just kidding around," Sean added. "What's your problem?"

"No problem," I replied, still cradling the camera.

Arjun raised his eyes to the darkening sky. Through the trees I could see only grey. "It's getting a bit late," Arjun murmured.

Sean's smile faded. "Let's get out of here." His eyes darted round the woods. Shadows deepened, and the air grew colder.

"They say some kind of wild creatures are loose in the woods," Arjun said softly.

"Arjun—give us a break," Hannah groaned, rolling her eyes.

"No. Really," Arjun insisted. "Some kind of creature tore off a deer's head. Tore it clean off."

"We saw it," Sean reported. His dark eyes glowed excitedly in the dimming light. "It was so gross!"

"The deer's eyes stared up at us," Arjun added. "And insects crawled out of its open neck."

"Yuck!" Hannah exclaimed, covering her mouth with one hand. "You're making this up—right?"

"No. I'm not." Sean glanced up at the moon.

"It's almost a full moon. The full moon makes all the strange creatures come out of hiding," he continued, speaking so softly, his voice just above a whisper. "Especially at Hallowe'en. And the moon will be completely full that night."

I shivered. The back of my neck tingled. I suddenly felt cold all over.

Was it the wind? Or Sean's frightening words?

I pictured the deer's head lying on the ground. Pictured the shiny black eyes staring up blankly, lifelessly.

"What are you going to be for Hallowe'en?" Arjun asked Hannah.

She shrugged. "I don't know. I haven't decided yet."

He turned to me. "Do you know what you want to be, Alex?"

I nodded. "Yeah. I want to be a werewolf."

Arjun uttered a near-silent gasp. The two boys exchanged glances.

Their smiles faded. Their faces turned solemn.

"What's wrong?" I asked.

No reply.

"Hey—what's wrong?" I repeated.

Arjun lowered his gaze to the ground. "We have enough werewolves in Wolf Creek," he murmured.

"What do you mean?" I cried. "Come on—what do you mean by that?"

But they didn't answer.

Instead, they turned and vanished into the woods.

Aunt Marta invited Hannah to stay for dinner. The four of us squeezed round the small kitchen table and spooned up big bowls of steaming chicken soup.

"You make great soup!" Hannah told my aunt.

Aunt Marta smiled. A little broth dripped down her chin. She reached for her napkin. "Thank you, Hannah. I just throw everything in it I can find."

"Sorry we were late for dinner," I said. "I lost track of time. I didn't want to leave the woods. It was so interesting."

Uncle Colin's eyes moved to the kitchen window. He stared up at the rising moon. Then he lowered his gaze to the Marlings' house next door.

"I photographed an awesome-looking tree," I told him. "It was wrinkled and bent over like an old man."

27

Uncle Colin didn't reply. His eyes were still focused out the window.

"Colin—Alex is talking to you," Aunt Marta scolded.

"Huh? Oh." He turned back to the table, shaking his head as if shaking away his thoughts. "Sorry. What were you saying?"

I told him again about the old tree.

"I'll help you develop those shots," he offered. "Maybe tomorrow. I've set up a darkroom in the little bathroom in the attic. We really need a bigger house. Especially with all the work we've been doing lately."

"What are you photographing now?" I asked.

"Creatures of the night," he replied. His eyes wandered to the window again. I followed his gaze to the Marlings' back window. Completely dark.

"We're photographing nocturnal animals," Aunt Marta explained. "Animals that come out only at night."

"You mean like owls?" Hannah asked.

Aunt Marta nodded. "We've found some wonderful owls in the woods—haven't we, Colin?"

Uncle Colin turned back from the window. Silvery light from the full moon washed over the window-pane. "The night creatures don't like to be photographed," he said, spooning up a carrot and chewing it slowly. "They are very private."

"Sometimes we wait in one spot for hours," my aunt added. "Waiting for a creature to poke its head up from its hole in the ground."

"Can I come with you one night?" I asked eagerly. "I can be very quiet. Really."

Uncle Colin swallowed a chunk of chicken. "That's a fine idea," he said. But then his expression grew solemn. And he added, "Maybe after Hallowe'en."

I turned and saw Aunt Marta staring out at the Marlings' house. "The moon is still low," she said thoughtfully. "But it's so bright tonight."

"Almost like daylight out there," Uncle Colin said. What was that expression that quickly passed over his face? Was it *fear*?

My aunt and uncle are both acting so weird tonight, I decided. So nervous.

Why do they keep staring out of the window? What do they expect to see at the Marlings' house?

I couldn't hold it in any longer. "Is everything okay?" I asked them.

"Okay?" Uncle Colin narrowed his eyes at me. "I suppose so . . ."

"Are you two thinking about your Hallowe'en costumes?" Aunt Marta demanded, changing the subject.

"I think I'm going to be a pirate again this year," Hannah replied. She finished her chocolate milk and licked the chocolate syrup on the

29

edge of the glass. "You know. I'll wrap a bandanna round my head and wear a patch over one eye."

"Colin and I might have some funny old clothes you can wear," Aunt Marta offered. She turned to me. "How about you, Alex?"

I still wanted to be a werewolf. But I remembered the last time I'd told that to my aunt and uncle. Uncle Colin had nearly crashed the van!

So I smiled and quietly told them. "Maybe I'll be a pirate too."

I spooned up the last of my soup.

I had no way of knowing that in a few hours, when the moon rose to its peak in the sky, I'd be nearly face to face with a *real* werewolf.

After Hannah had gone home, I made my way to my little bedroom. I tidied up a bit, shoving clothes into the dresser drawers.

I'm not the neatest person in the world. Let's face it—I'm a slob. But I knew if I let the clutter pile up in this tiny room, I'd never find anything.

I sat down at the desk and wrote a short letter to Mum and Dad. I told them everything was fine. I wrote that I'd have at least a thousand great photographs to show them when they came home from France.

When I finished addressing the letter, I wasn't feeling sleepy. But I decided I should probably go to bed anyway.

I moved towards the wardrobe to find my pyjamas. But I stopped at the window.

And stared out at a pale orange light.

A light in a side window of the Marlings' house!

The light shimmered between two tilting

31

trees, their leaves vibrating in the wind. A pale orange rectangle of light on the bottom floor of the house, near the back.

A bedroom window?

I pressed closer to the glass and squinted hard into the darkness. Squinted into the dim rectangle of orange.

Was I about to see one of the Marlings? I held my breath and waited.

I didn't have to wait long.

I let out a gasp as a silhouette crossed the window next door. A grey figure caught in the rectangle of orange.

Was it a man?

I couldn't tell.

The silhouette moved. It's an animal, I realized.

No. A man.

Mr Marling?

I pressed against the glass, squinting hard. Was it a large dog? A man? I couldn't see clearly.

The silhouette moved away from the window.

And then I heard a long, high animal wail.

The sound floated out through the window next door. Floated across the narrow space between our houses.

The high, animal howl swept into my room. Swirled round me.

Such an ugly, frightening sound. Half-human, half-animal. A cry I had never heard before.

A chill rolled down my back. And then another.

Another howl made me gasp.

I stared out as the silhouette returned to the window. A creature with its head tilted back. Its jaws open, uttering such frightening animal cries.

I've got to take a picture, I told myself. I've got to photograph the howling silhouette.

I spun away from the window. Dived across the tiny room to the dresser.

Reached for my camera.

My camera?

It had gone.

"No—!" I uttered a shocked cry.

My hands fumbled frantically over the desktop.

I had left the camera there. I knew I had.

But no. No camera.

My eyes swept round the room. I had just tidied up. Everything was in place. The desktop. The dresser.

No camera. No camera.

I dropped to my knees and searched under the bed.

No camera.

I crawled over to the wardrobe. Pulled open the door. And searched the wardrobe floor.

As I searched, another wolf howl burst into my room. Higher. Shriller.

And then I heard two howls together. The siren-like wails blending in a strange, sour harmony.

Was it Mr and Mrs Marling?

As I climbed to my feet, I heard a scraping sound. Wood against wood.

The sound of a window opening.

I heard a heavy *THUD*.

Feet landing hard on the ground.

And then I heard low grunts. Heavy, thudding footsteps.

Footsteps right outside my room!

I dived back to the window. Breathlessly, my heart pounding, I stared out.

Too late.

No one out there now.

All dark. The orange light gone from the Marlings' window. The house completely covered in black again.

The trees shaking, black against the blue-black sky. The leaves silvery, shimmering under the bright light of the moon.

I stared out there for a long moment, waiting for my heart to stop racing. Listening for the high howls, the heavy, thudding footsteps.

Silence now.

My camera . . .

I forced myself to turn away from the window. I hurried out of the room and down the short hall to the living-room. Had I left the camera case here when Hannah and I returned from the woods?

No. No sign of it.

I checked the kitchen. Not there, either.

"Aunt Marta! Uncle Colin!" I called them. My voice came out tinier than I'd planned.

I ran back down the hall. Past my room. Past the bathroom and the linen cupboard. Their room stood at the end. "Have you seen my camera anywhere?" I cried.

I shoved open the door to their bedroom.

Dark in there. Dark and empty.

I could smell Aunt Marta's flowery perfume. And the sharp odour of photo-developing fluid.

They've gone out to the woods to photograph animals, I realized.

I'm all alone here.

I took a deep breath and held it. Calm down, Alex, I instructed myself. You're perfectly okay. You're perfectly safe.

You will find your camera as soon as you get calm. It's probably right out in plain sight. But you're so crazy and pumped up, you can't see it. Just calm down!

I took another long, deep breath. I was starting to feel calmer.

I closed my aunt and uncle's bedroom door and started back down the hall.

I was halfway to my room when I heard the soft, scraping sound.

And then the thud of footsteps.

I froze. And listened.

More footsteps. Heavy thuds.

Where were they coming from?

Overhead?

Yes.

I peered up at the low ceiling.

Another scraping sound. More thudding footsteps.

They're in the attic! I realized.

Whatever those howling creatures are— *they're in the house!*

I dropped back against the wall. My whole body shook.

I swallowed hard. And listened to the heavy footsteps above my head.

I've got to get out of here! I told myself. I've got to get out of this house!

I've got to tell Uncle Colin and Aunt Marta!

But my legs felt like jelly. I didn't know if I could walk.

I took a shaky step. Then another.

And then I heard a new sound from upstairs.

I stopped and listened.

Humming? Was someone *humming*?

With a burst of energy, I grabbed the door to the attic. I pulled it open and shouted up the stairs, "Who's up there? Who is it?"

"It's me, Alex!" a familiar voice called down.

"Hannah—?" I choked out. I stared up at the attic. "Wh-what are you doing up there?"

"Didn't your aunt tell you I came back?" Hannah called.

"No, she didn't," I replied.

"She said she had some old clothes up here that might make a good costume. So I came back to check it out."

Her head appeared at the top of the stairs. "Why do you sound so weird?"

"I—I thought—" I began. But the words caught in my throat.

I started up the stairs.

"No—!" Hannah cried. "Don't come up!"

I stopped on the third step. "How come?" I called.

"I'm not dressed. I'm trying on stuff," she explained. She smiled down at me. "Besides, I want to surprise you. There's some *awesome* old stuff up here. Your aunt and uncle must have looked really *weird* when they were young."

Her head disappeared from view. I could hear the rustle of clothes up there.

I backed down the stairs. "Hey—do you know where my camera is?" I asked. "I've looked all over the house, and—"

"Oh, no!" Hannah groaned. Her head appeared again. This time she wasn't smiling.

"What?" I called up to her.

"Your camera, Alex. Do you think you could have left it in the woods?"

I gasped. "I don't know. I thought . . ." My

voice trailed off. I had a sick, heavy feeling in the pit of my stomach.

"You had it when Sean and Arjun left," Hannah said. "But when we came back to the house, I don't remember you carrying it."

"Oh, wow!" I shook my head. "I've got to go and get it, Hannah. I can't leave it overnight in the woods."

"*No—!*" she cried. "Alex, listen to me. You can't go out there."

"I have to!" I cried.

"But the woods aren't safe at night," she protested. "They really aren't safe."

I turned away and ran down the hall. I pulled on my jacket and found a torch on the floor of the hall cupboard. I tested it a few times. The light was steady and bright.

"I'll be back in a few minutes," I shouted up to Hannah.

"No—please, Alex!" I heard her call down. "Listen to me! Don't go into the woods tonight! Wait for me to get dressed. Just wait for me—okay?"

But I couldn't leave my camera out there to be ruined.

I closed the front door behind me and stepped out into the light of the moon.

I began trotting along the side of the house towards the back garden. Heavy black clouds covered the moon. The night air felt colder than I'd thought. Wet. I zipped up my down jacket as I ran.

I glanced at the Marlings' house as I jogged past. Nothing to see there. The back window had been left wide open. But the house was completely dark. Not a light on anywhere.

The grass was slick and wet from a heavy dew. I felt a splash of cold on my forehead.

A raindrop?

I groaned as I thought of my camera, sitting out in the woods. It was such an expensive camera. I prayed I could find it before it started to rain.

Several tiny animals scampered silently past my feet.

I stopped.

No. Not animals. Fat, dead leaves. They scuttled over the dark grass, pushed by swirls of wind.

I lowered my head under a tree branch and entered the woods at the back of the garden. The old trees shivered and creaked.

The steady *WHOO* of an owl, far in the distance, made me think of my aunt and uncle. They were here with their cameras somewhere in the woods. I wondered if I would run into them.

I followed the twisting path through the trees. Another raindrop fell heavily on the top of my head. Rain spattered the ground.

I stopped when the bent tree came into view. The tree I had photographed with Hannah that afternoon. I played my torch over its curved shape.

"At least I'm heading in the right direction," I said out loud.

I stepped over a fallen branch and moved deeper into the woods. The trees began to hiss, the leaves shaking in the rising wind. I could still hear the owl's steady *WHOO WHOO* in the distance.

My torch dimmed, then brightened again. Its thin circle of light made a path for me between the trees.

"All right!"

I cried out when the light swept over my

camera case. I had set it down on a flat tree stump. How could I have forgotten it there?

With another happy cry, I picked it up. I actually felt like hugging it. I was so happy to have it back. I checked it out carefully, turning it under the torch.

I wiped away the few raindrops that clung to the top. Then, cradling it under one arm, I started back to the house.

The rain had stopped, at least for a moment. I started to hum happily. I wanted to *skip* all the way home!

The camera meant more to me than anything. I promised myself I'd never leave it anywhere again.

I stopped humming when I heard the angry sound.

An animal snarl. A fierce, throaty roar.

I dropped the torch.

The creature roared again.

Where was it? Where was it coming from?

Right behind me!

I bent and grabbed up the torch. My knees suddenly felt weak. A cold wave of panic swept over my body.

I heard loud animal grunts. Another angry snarl.

I forced myself to move. I had to get away from there.

A clump of fat shrubs rose up in front of me. Clutching my camera case, I darted behind them. And dropped to my knees.

Hidden beneath the bushes, I struggled to catch my breath. To stop my heart from thudding so hard in my chest.

I couldn't see round the fat leaves of the bush. But I could hear the animal's grunts and growls. I ducked lower, hoping I was completely out of view.

Hoping it couldn't *smell* me.

And then I heard the crash of heavy feet on

the ground. A high wail of anger, like a cry of attack.

A frightened bleat rose up. So high and tiny. A terrified cry—cut off quickly.

Snapped off.

Leaning into the shrub, my legs trembling, my whole body shaking, I heard a struggle.

So close. So close, I felt I could stand up—reach out—and touch the attacker and his prey.

So close, I heard every grunt, every frightened cry.

A thud. A growl. Another tiny, helpless bleat.

A loud ripping sound.

Wet chewing. The slap of jaws. More rapid chewing. An animal burp. Another ripping sound.

I shut my eyes, picturing what was happening right in front of me.

I heard a thud. Then silence.

The hiss of the wind seemed to grow louder.

A hiss . . . then silence.

I opened my eyes.

I stood up shakily.

And heard heavy footsteps. Twigs and leaves crackling under heavy feet.

The footsteps approaching rapidly. Coming my way.

Coming for *me*. The creature—the hungry creature—was moving towards me.

"Ohhhh." A low cry of terror escaped my throat.

Gripping the camera case tightly, I spun away from the clump of shrubs. And started to run.

I heard animal grunts behind me. Heavy-breathing pants.

I didn't glance back.

I ran deeper into the woods. I thought I heard the splash and trickle of a creek on my right. Wolf Creek? I didn't stop to see.

A branch scratched my cheek as I scrambled past it. Pain shot over my face.

I raised one arm to shield myself as I ran.

Ran blindly. Ran through the darkness.

Where was the torch?

Oh, no. I'd left it behind in the bushes.

It was of no use to me, anyway. I was running too fast to keep to the path.

I lowered my shoulder and pushed my way through a patch of tall reeds. They snapped back, slapping me wetly as I shot through them.

My foot caught on a half-buried rock. I slid off it, somehow keeping my balance.

I leapt over an upraised tree root—and kept running.

Over the harsh gasps of my breath, I listened for the heavy, thudding footsteps behind me. The animal growls.

Was the creature still chasing me?

I grabbed a smooth, damp tree trunk and

stopped. I hugged the trunk, struggling to keep my legs from collapsing, struggling to catch my breath.

I turned and gazed back.

Nothing there.

No growls. No grunts. No bang of heavy feet on the ground.

I sucked in breath after breath. My lungs burned. My mouth felt so dry, I couldn't swallow.

I'm okay, I told myself. I'm safe—for now.

I gazed into the deep darkness.

And the creature hit me from behind.

"Hunh—!"

I uttered a startled groan. And dropped to the ground.

I spun round to face my attacker.

No one there.

Nothing.

"Huh?" A shocked cry escaped my lips.

I started to scramble to my feet—and saw what had hit the back of my head.

A bird's nest. A dried-up, broken bird's nest. It must have fallen from a branch above my head. Probably shaken loose by the gusts of wind.

"Oh, wow." I shook twigs from my hair. Then, cradling the camera case under my arm, I gazed round.

Where was I?

Trees up ahead slanted as if leaning against each other. A low mound of rocks stood at the edge of a ridge of tall reeds.

I'm lost, I realized.

I gazed up at the sky. No moon. The heavy rain clouds covered the moon and stars.

How do I get back? I squinted into the darkness, searching for the path. Searching for anything I might recognize.

Nothing.

If I could find the creek, maybe I could find the spot where I found my camera, I decided.

But which direction was the creek?

I was completely disorientated.

I shivered. A cold raindrop spattered on the shoulder of my jacket.

I jumped. That bird's nest had made me terrified of things falling from the sky!

What should I do?

My mind whirred frantically with ideas.

Should I call out for help? Shout to my aunt and uncle? Maybe if I called loud enough, they would hear me.

But no. If I shout, the animal—the snarling creature—will hear me first.

Was it still searching for me? Was it still nearby?

I decided I'd better not call for help.

What should I do? *What?*

Start walking in one direction? And just keep going no matter what?

No. I remembered a book I'd read where a man was lost in the desert. And he tried walking in a straight line. And he just made circles. He went round and round and didn't even realize it until he saw his own footprints in the sand!

Maybe I should wait until the sun comes up, I decided. I'll never find my way in this darkness. When it's daylight, I'll have a much better chance.

I didn't like the idea of spending the night in the woods. But waiting here until I could see where I was going seemed like a good idea.

But then I heard a clattering sound. And felt the rain start to pound down hard. A freezing rain, swept by gusting wind.

I can't stay here, I realized.

I have to get back to the house.

I walked and walked, trying to retrace my steps. I sighed with relief when I finally came to the clump of bushes where I'd hidden. I found the torch and gripped it tightly in my free hand.

I took a guess on which direction to go next.

Ducking my head against the rain, I started to walk again.

Less than a minute later, I stumbled over something.

Something soft.

I landed on my knees. Turned back to see what I had tripped over.

And let out a cry of horror.

The torch trembled in my hand. The quivering light revealed an ugly picture.

I gaped down at an animal body. No. Two.

Two animals.

What were they? I couldn't tell. They'd been clawed to pieces.

Completely ripped apart.

I remembered the ripping sounds I'd heard. The sounds of these animals being torn apart. My stomach lurched.

What kind of animal had done this?

What kind of animal was strong enough to tear other creatures apart?

A chill ran down my back.

I pulled myself to my feet. I forced myself to look away.

The rain poured down. I shielded my camera case under my jacket—and started to run again.

I had to get away from that ugly sight. Would I ever be able to forget it?

The wind whipped the rain round me. I felt as if I were running through ocean waves. But I couldn't stop.

My fear kept me running.

That fierce creature still lurked in these woods. Still growled and hunted, somewhere nearby.

My trainers were soaked. I slipped and slid in the soft mud.

I'm not sure how long I ran. I stopped when I nearly ran right into the creek. Pounded by the rain, it splashed over its low bank.

I turned and followed it, feeling a little more confident. After a while, I spotted a narrow path cut through the tilting trees.

I turned on to the path. Would it lead me out of the woods? I had to try it.

The rain slowed to a soft patter. My trainers sank deep into the mud as I trotted along the curving path.

Soon I came to the bent, old-man tree.

"Yes!" I cried out loud. "Yes!" I waved my fist triumphantly in the air. I was almost home.

I picked up my pace. A few minutes later, I burst out of the woods, into my aunt and uncle's back garden.

I was so happy! I wanted to fly!

I couldn't wait to get into the warm house. To pull off my soaked clothes and get into something dry.

But I stopped in the middle of the garden.

And stared into the circle of yellow light from my torch.

Stared down at the strange footprints in the wet grass.

Deep, rutted footprints heading into the Marlings' back garden.

I bent into the light to see them better. They weren't human footprints. They were too long and too wide and shaped differently from human feet or shoes.

Animal footprints.

Keeping the beam of light in front of me, I trailed the footprints, following them over the grass.

Across the Marlings' weed-choked garden.

I stopped when I saw where the strange footprints led.

Right up to the Marlings' open bedroom window.

When I came into the kitchen for breakfast the next morning, Aunt Marta was on the phone. She stood at the worktop with her back to me. But she turned as I said good morning to my uncle, and flashed me an angry look.

"Yes, I understand," she said into the phone. "Well, it won't happen again."

I took my place at the table beside Uncle Colin. He sipped from a white coffee mug, his eyes on Aunt Marta.

"It won't happen again," my aunt repeated into the phone. She frowned. "I'll make sure he stays away. No. He wasn't *spying* on you, Mr Marling."

So *that's* who she was talking to.

Uncle Colin shook his head unhappily. "I warned you not to go near that place, Alex," he said. "We don't need those people calling over here."

"Sorry," I murmured. "But—"

I wanted to tell him about last night, about everything that had happened to me and everything I'd seen.

But he raised a finger to his lips, motioning for me to be silent while my aunt was on the phone.

"No. My nephew wasn't taking pictures of your house, Mr Marling," Aunt Marta continued. She rolled her eyes. "I promise. He won't bother you again. I'll talk to him right now. Yes. Okay. Goodbye."

She set down the receiver and turned to Uncle Colin with a sigh. "Those people," she murmured.

"We have to be careful," Uncle Colin replied, narrowing his eyes at me. "We don't want to get them worked up."

"But—but—" I sputtered. "I *saw* things—"

"They saw *you*, Alex," my aunt interrupted. "They saw you prowling round their house late last night. They are *very* angry about it."

She poured herself a mug of coffee and came over to the table. She sat down and swept a strand of grey hair off her forehead.

"What were you doing outside last night?" my uncle asked.

"I'm really sorry. But I had no choice. I'd left my camera out in the woods," I explained. "I had to run out and get it. I couldn't leave it out all night—especially with the rain."

"But you didn't have to go near the Marlings' house—did you?" Aunt Marta demanded.

"I—I heard animal howls from inside their house!" I blurted out. "And I saw strange footprints going up to the bedroom window at the side."

Uncle Colin nodded calmly. He took a long sip of coffee. "The footprints were probably from their dogs," he said, glancing at Aunt Marta.

"Dogs?" I cried.

They both nodded. "They have two huge Alsatians," my aunt explained. "Mean as they come."

"And as big as wolves," Uncle Colin added, shaking his head. He reached for a slice of toast and began to butter it.

I sighed. I felt a little better.

Two Alsatians. That explained the howls and the footprints in the wet grass.

"Are you ready for school?" Aunt Marta asked. "Hannah will be here any minute."

"I'm almost ready," I replied. I gulped down a glass of orange juice. "When I was in the woods last night . . ." I started.

They both stared at me.

"I saw some animals that had been ripped up. I mean, killed."

Uncle Colin nodded. "The woods are dangerous at night," he said softly.

"We really don't want you out there at night, Alex," Aunt Marta said. She pulled a piece of lint off the shoulder of my T-shirt. Then she tenderly brushed my hair back with her hand. "Promise us you won't go again."

"Promise," I murmured.

"And promise that you'll stay away from the Marlings," my uncle added.

Before I could reply, the doorbell rang. Hannah came into the kitchen, weighted down under a bulging rucksack. "Ready?" she asked.

I nodded and shoved my chair back from the table. "Yeah. I think I'm ready," I told her. "This is so weird. Going to someone else's school."

"You'll like my teacher, Mr Shein," Hannah replied. "He's very interesting. And he's really nice."

I grabbed my rucksack and my jacket. We said goodbye to my aunt and uncle and headed out of the front door.

I glanced at the Marlings' house as we made our way to the street. The bedroom window at the side had been closed, I saw. The house was as dark as always.

"Did you find your camera?" Hannah asked.

I nodded. "Yeah. But it wasn't easy." I told her about my scary adventures.

She *tsk-tsk*ed. "I warned you, Alex," she said. "You wouldn't catch *me* in the woods after dark."

A yellow school bus rumbled past. Some kids in the bus called out of the window to Hannah. She waved back to them.

The morning sun still floated low in the sky. A silvery frost clung to the lawns. The air felt crisp and cold.

"One more block to school," Hannah said. "Are you nervous?"

I didn't answer. I was thinking about the Marlings. I told Hannah about the howls I'd heard inside their house. "Uncle Colin says they have two Alsatians. Really big and really mean," I told her.

"No, they don't," Hannah replied sharply.

I stopped walking. "Excuse me?" I cried.

"The Marlings don't have any dogs," she repeated. "I've lived here as long as they have, and I've never seen them."

"Then why did my uncle tell me that?" I demanded.

"So you won't be scared," Hannah replied.

"I—I don't understand," I stammered. "If the Marlings don't have dogs, what made those weird footprints outside their window?"

Hannah shook her head. Her olive-green eyes locked on to mine. "Alex, don't you get it?" she cried. "Haven't you figured it out yet?"

"Figured *what* out?" I asked.

"The Marlings are werewolves!" Hannah declared.

Why is everyone in Wolf Creek *obsessed* with werewolves? I wondered.

I laughed at Hannah and teased her for the rest of the walk to school. I mean, how could anyone actually believe in werewolves today?

"You're only trying to scare me," I told her. "But I don't scare easily—remember? I saw one of the Alsatians. It was howling in the Marlings' window."

Hannah shrugged. "Believe what you want to believe," she murmured.

"Don't try to scare me with werewolves any more," I told her.

But I had a surprise when we arrived at school. Even Mr Shein, the sixth-grade teacher, wanted to talk about werewolves all morning!

He was about forty, short and chubby, with thinning brown hair and thick black glasses perched on his round pink face. He wore a yellow sweater that made him resemble a ripe pear.

But Hannah was right. He was very nice. Very friendly. He welcomed me eagerly and introduced me to the other sixth graders, and really made me feel at home.

He assigned me a seat near the door at the back. Hannah sat in the front row.

I spotted Sean and Arjun near the windows on the other side of the classroom. They nodded, but didn't say hi or anything.

They both looked rumpled and a bit tired. Their baggy clothes were very wrinkled. Their hair was wild. They look as if they've been up all night, I thought.

Weird thought . . .

After taking the register and making a few announcements, Mr Shein sat on the edge of his desk. His eyes travelled round the room. He waited for us to settle down.

"Does anyone know what lycanthropy is?" he asked. Behind his glasses, his dark eyes glowed.

I had never heard the word. But to my surprise, several hands shot up. He called on Arjun.

"It's about people changing into wolves," Arjun said.

"Werewolves!" Sean exclaimed.

Mr Shein nodded. "Yes. Werewolves," he repeated. "That's what lycanthropy is about." He cleared his throat. "Since Hallowe'en comes

60

later this week, I thought we might spend some time discussing lycanthropy."

"There is going to be a full moon on Hallowe'en night this year!" a tall, athletic-looking boy interrupted.

"Yes, there is," Mr Shein agreed. "Many people believe a full moon is needed to bring the werewolf to life—but they are wrong. Although a werewolf's powers *do* grow stronger as the moon grows fuller."

Crossing his legs, he leant back and began to talk. He explained how the werewolf legends began over two hundred years ago in Europe. A normal person, bitten by a werewolf, becomes a werewolf himself when moonlight shines on him.

"It is a curse that cannot be removed," Mr Shein said, speaking in a low, steady voice. Trying to sound spooky. "No matter how much he tries to live a normal life, a man inflicted with the curse turns into a wolf under the light of the moon."

"Girls too?" Hannah asked.

Some kids giggled.

"Yes. Girls too," the teacher answered seriously.

"The werewolf must rage and howl," Mr Shein continued. "And prowl the woods or forest in search of victims."

"Cool!" a red-haired boy in front of me muttered.

61

Everyone laughed.

"At daybreak, the werewolves must shed their wolfskin," the teacher explained. "They return to human form. They must hide their wolfskin until the next night. They must hide the skin in a safe place. Because if someone takes the werewolf's skin and burns it . . . the werewolf will die."

"Cool!" the red-haired boy repeated.

More laughter. Kids started talking excitedly.

It took a while for Mr Shein to quieten everyone. He jumped to his feet, pulled down his yellow sweater, and paced in front of the blackboard.

"Does anyone in this class believe that werewolves really exist?" he asked.

I sniggered. I didn't think any kids would raise their hands.

But to my surprise, *every single hand in the room* shot up.

"You *all* believe in werewolves!" Mr Shein declared.

"Yes, we do," I heard Arjun murmur softly.

"Yes, we do," Sean repeated.

I turned and realized they were both staring hard at me.

I felt a sudden chill. What is their problem? I wondered. Why are they acting so weird?

After school, Sean and Arjun came up to me at the back of the classroom. Outside the room, lockers slammed. The tile walls echoed with shouts and laughter.

The two guys studied me solemnly. "What's up?" I greeted them, zipping up my rucksack.

Mr Shein waved and walked out, carrying a bulging briefcase. The three of us were alone in the room.

"How's it going?" Sean asked.

"Is it weird being in a new school?" Arjun said.

"Yeah. A bit," I told them. "Especially since I know I'm only here for a few weeks."

"You're lucky!" Arjun joked. "Sean and I are stuck here."

"Wolf Creek isn't that bad," I said. I swung the rucksack on to my shoulder.

The two boys stared at me intently. They didn't say anything. Sean shoved his hands into his baggy jeans pockets. Arjun fiddled with a silver ring on his little finger.

Finally, Sean broke the silence. "You don't believe in werewolves," he said softly.

"Huh? Well . . ." I hesitated.

"You didn't raise your hand," Arjun added. "Everyone else did."

"Yeah. I know," I replied. "I really don't believe in them. I mean, come on. It's practically the twenty-first century. See a lot of men with fur on their faces walking round the streets? I don't think so!"

I meant it to be funny. But they didn't laugh. They kept staring at me with their solemn faces.

"Werewolves exist," Arjun said softly. "We can prove it to you."

"Sure," I replied sarcastically, rolling my eyes. "The Easter Bunny exists too. I saw him riding a bus in Cleveland."

"We can prove it to you, Alex," Arjun insisted. "We can show you a werewolf."

"A real one," Sean added.

"No, thanks," I said. "I really—"

"You can take pictures of it," Arjun interrupted.

"Yeah. You can take a whole roll!" his friend cried.

That made me stop and think. I remembered the photography competition I was planning to enter. I needed a Hallowe'en photo—a really good Hallowe'en photo—for the competition.

They moved closer, surrounding me, forcing me to back up until I bumped into the window-sill.

"Want to see a real werewolf, Alex?" Sean demanded.

"Want to take photos of a real werewolf?" Arjun asked.

They stared hard at me, challenging me.

"What do I have to do?" I asked.

Aunt Marta laughed. "Hannah—you look *dreadful*!" she cried, pressing her hands against her cheeks.

"Thank you!" Hannah took a low bow. "Thank you!"

After dinner, Hannah had come over to show off her Hallowe'en costume. She'd changed her mind about dressing as a pirate. The costume she chose instead was hard to describe. She had taken a lot of old clothes, torn them all up, and sewn them back together.

Her baggy trousers had one brown leg and one green leg. And they had checked patches at the knees. She wore a ragged shirt of yellow, blue, red—every colour you can imagine. An even more colourful jacket over the shirt. And a floppy rag hat that kept falling over her face.

"What are you supposed to be?" I asked. "A junkyard?"

She didn't laugh. "I'm a rag doll," she replied. "Don't you get it?" She tugged at the jacket. "Rags?"

Aunt Marta and Uncle Colin both laughed. I was happy to see them enjoying themselves. They had both seemed tired and low at dinner. They had barely spoken to me.

"There used to be a song about a rag doll," Aunt Marta said. "Remember it, Colin?"

My uncle shook his head. "I don't remember anything any more," he replied. "I'm lucky if I remember to get up in the morning!"

"Oh, give me a break, Colin!" Aunt Marta scolded. She gave him a playful shove. She began singing a song about a rag doll.

Hannah did a silly dance, twirling her hands above her head. One of her jacket sleeves fell off, and we all laughed.

"Where's your costume, Alex?" my aunt demanded. "Go and put it on. Come on. Let's have a preview."

"I—I haven't put one together yet," I stammered.

"Well, let's get some old clothes and make you a costume tonight!" Aunt Marta insisted.

"No. I . . . need to think about it," I told her.

I didn't have my mind on costumes. I kept glancing out of the front window at the darkening sky. Thinking about what I planned to do later.

I planned to meet Sean and Arjun in the

woods by the creek. At school, they'd told me to take my camera and meet them there.

They'd said that the werewolf comes to that spot every night when the moon is at its highest point in the sky. "It howls up at the moon," Arjun had said in an excited whisper. "And then it lowers its head and laps up water from the creek."

"Wait till you see it!" Sean had exclaimed. "It's a man and a wolf at the same time. He's half-human, half-animal."

I'd narrowed my eyes at the two of them. I'd tried to decide if they were joking or not. Their expressions had been so serious—and so excited—I had decided they were telling the truth.

Was it possible? Did werewolves really exist?

I pictured the howling creature in the Marlings' window. And I pictured the two animals in the woods, ripped to pieces.

By a werewolf?

The back of my neck tingled. I'd never believed in werewolves. But I'd seldom been out of the city.

Here in this small town surrounded by woods, they began to seem real.

"Will you meet us at midnight?" Sean had asked.

I didn't want to return to the woods at night. Not after what I'd seen there.

But I didn't want them to know I was afraid.

And I really needed a great photo to win the

competition. A photo of a werewolf would definitely win! What else could come close?

So I'd agreed to sneak out of the house and meet Sean and Arjun at midnight in the woods. But now, as it grew later, I began to feel really nervous about it.

As I glanced out at the darkness beyond the window, I had a heavy feeling in the pit of my stomach. And my hands were suddenly cold and clammy.

"Alex, what are you thinking about?" Aunt Marta's voice broke into my thoughts.

"Huh?" I blinked and shook my head.

Everyone laughed. "You were staring out of the window with the strangest look on your face," Hannah declared.

"Oh. Just watching the moon," I said with a shrug.

"It's Moon Madness!" Uncle Colin joked. "*OOOH.* Looks like a bad case!"

"What's that?" I asked.

"How should I know?" my uncle replied. "I've just made it up!"

We all laughed again.

Everyone was in such a good mood. I wished I could relax and have fun too. But all I could think about was sneaking out to the woods.

Hannah went home a short while later. I said good-night to my aunt and uncle and closed myself up in my room.

I glanced at the bedside clock. It read ten fifteen.

Nearly two hours to wait.

I checked my camera. Made sure I had it loaded with high-speed film.

Then I sat down to read a photography magazine—and wait—hoping the time would pass quickly.

My eyes stared at the pages of the magazine. But I couldn't read. I couldn't concentrate.

Every few seconds, my eyes went to the clock.

Why does time move so slowly when you're waiting?

Finally, at about ten to midnight, I closed my magazine. Pulled on an extra sweater and then my jacket. I grabbed my camera case and slung the strap over my shoulder.

Then I tiptoed to the bedroom door.

My aunt and uncle were probably out in the woods, photographing night animals. But in case they'd decided to stay in tonight, I didn't want them to hear me sneak out.

I clicked off the lights in my room. Then I reached for the doorknob and tugged.

"Hey—!"

I turned the knob and tugged again.

I turned it the other way and gave the door a hard jerk.

"I don't believe it!" I gasped.

I'd been locked in.

The door must be stuck, I decided.

I tugged it hard. Tugged it a dozen times. I even tried *pushing*. But I couldn't budge it. It had definitely been locked, locked from the outside.

I angrily spun away from the door.

Why did my aunt and uncle lock me in? I wondered. Because of last night? Because of my close calls in the woods?

"They can't do this to me!" I exclaimed.

I ran to the window. I jerked the curtains apart and reached for the window handles.

The window slid up a few centimetres—and I let out a gasp.

Metal bars had been installed outside.

When did they put those on? This afternoon?

I'm a prisoner! I told myself. I'm locked in this room like an animal in a cage!

"They can't do this to me!" I repeated. "They can't!"

I slid the window up all the way. I grabbed the metal bars with both hands and struggled to prise them loose.

But they wouldn't budge.

I was still tugging on the bars when I heard a low growl.

My hands dropped away, and a sharp cry escaped my throat.

I froze.

And heard another growl. Louder this time.

And close. So close.

A shrill howl rose up. From the Marlings' house?

I moved my face up close to the bars and peered out. Their bedroom window stood open again. But the house was completely dark. No lights anywhere.

I squinted into the darkness. The moon had disappeared behind a cloud. I could barely see across to their house.

Pressed against the bars, I heard an animal grunt. And then a thud.

A dark shape dropped down from the Marlings' open window. Another thud. Another shape dropped down on all fours.

One of the creatures raised its head in a long, mournful howl.

And then they took off, loping heavily towards the back garden, heading for the woods.

Dogs? Wolves? Humans?

I couldn't see clearly in the darkness.

I stared out, and a silvery light washed over the house as the cloud drifted away from the moon.

But now it was too late. Too late.

The creatures had vanished.

I pounded the bars with my fists.

Sean and Arjun were waiting for me by the creek. And there was no way I could get there.

What would they think? That I was a total chicken? A wimp?

I'm missing my big chance to take a winning photograph! I realized.

Angrily, I slammed the window shut.

"Tomorrow night!" I declared out loud. "Tomorrow night I'm getting out of here. My aunt and uncle won't stop me.

"Tomorrow night I'm going into the woods, and I'm going to find out the truth about werewolves!"

"How could you do that to me?" I shrieked. I burst into the kitchen for breakfast the next morning, and strode angrily up to my aunt and uncle.

"How could you lock me in my room without telling me?" I cried.

Aunt Marta set down her coffee mug. She gazed up at me with a troubled expression. Then she turned to Uncle Colin. "Maybe we should have told Alex," she said.

Uncle Colin narrowed his eyes at me. "Did you try to get out last night, Alex?"

"Well..." I hesitated. I didn't want to tell them what I had planned to do. "I don't like being in a cage!" I protested. "I'm twelve years old and I really think—"

"We're sorry," Aunt Marta interrupted. She glanced at the kitchen clock and poured me out a bowl of corn flakes.

"But we did it for your own good," Uncle Colin added. He folded his napkin tensely between his hands. "We had no choice. We can't let you go running out to the woods the way you did your first night. It just isn't safe."

"We're responsible for you," Aunt Marta said, pushing the cereal bowl across the table to me. "We promised your parents we'd return you safe and sound. We don't want to lock you in, Alex. But we have to make sure—"

"But—but—" I sputtered.

"Besides, the Marlings called the police yesterday," Uncle Colin said, frowning.

"They *what*?" I cried. "They called the police—about *me*?"

He nodded. "They complained about you spying on them," he said.

I let out an angry scream. "That's really stupid!" I cried. "I didn't spy on them! I didn't do anything to them!"

"Okay, okay." Aunt Marta came round the table and placed a comforting hand on my shoulder. "Don't worry about the Marlings. Just don't go anywhere near their house—okay?"

I turned to her. "Are they werewolves?" I blurted out.

Uncle Colin gasped.

Aunt Marta uttered a short laugh. "Is that what Hannah told you?" she demanded.

"Well . . . yes," I replied.

She shook her head. "Hannah has a twisted sense of humour," she said.

"The Marlings are just very odd, very unfriendly people," Uncle Colin told me. He glanced out of the kitchen window towards their house. And added: "Two unfriendly people with two *very* unfriendly dogs."

"Hannah said they don't have any dogs," I insisted.

Uncle Colin made a disgusted face. "Tell your friend Hannah to stop pulling your leg."

"What do you mean?" I asked.

"She's trying to scare you, Alex. Don't listen to her."

The doorbell rang. Hannah had arrived to walk me to school.

I was happy to get out of the house. I still felt angry about being locked up.

As we walked to school, I didn't tell Hannah about it. I knew she'd probably think it was funny. And she'd tell other kids about how my aunt and uncle were so worried about me, they locked me in like a baby.

I didn't mention the Marlings' dogs, either. I didn't want to get into another argument about werewolves. I wanted to find out the truth for myself.

At school, I hung my jacket in my locker and headed for Mr Shein's class. But as I turned the corner, Sean and Arjun stepped up to block my path.

They'd been waiting for me. They moved

quickly to back me against the wall. Their eyes glowed with excitement.

"Hey, Alex." Sean poked me in the shoulder.

"Seen any *werewolves* lately?" Arjun demanded.

"Uh . . . well . . ." I didn't know what to say. "You see . . . my aunt and uncle . . ."

Why were they staring at me like that? Were they trying to scare me?

A strange grin spread over Sean's face. "Have a good time in the woods last night?" he asked.

"Yeah. How was it?" Arjun demanded. "Catch any werewolves, Alex?"

I bumped them off me and stepped away from the wall. "You mean you weren't there?" I cried.

They both burst out laughing. They slapped each other a high five.

"Of course not!" Arjun declared. "Why would we go into the woods in the middle of the night?"

"I was sound asleep by midnight," Sean said, grinning.

They laughed and congratulated each other again.

A joke. The whole thing had been a joke. They

hadn't waited for me in the woods at midnight. They had never intended to go to the woods.

"So how was it?" Sean asked. "Were you surprised when Arjun and I didn't show up?"

"No. I didn't even think of you," I told them. "Do you know why? Because I was too busy taking photos of the werewolf!"

"Huh?" Sean cried.

It was *their* turn to be surprised.

Of course I was lying. But they had no way of knowing that I hadn't gone to the woods, either.

"What did you see?" Arjun asked suspiciously.

"I followed a werewolf," I told him, forcing myself not to crack a smile. "He came to the creek and he drank, just as you said."

"Give me a break," Sean groaned.

"Yeah. Really!" Arjun rolled his eyes. "In your dreams."

"I can prove it. I took a whole roll of film," I told them.

"Let's see the pictures," Sean demanded.

"I haven't developed them yet," I replied.

They stared at me, trying to decide if I was telling the truth. I felt a laugh about to explode inside me. But somehow I kept a straight face.

The bell rang.

"We're late!" Arjun cried.

The three of us bolted down the hall to the room. We dived into our seats two seconds before Mr Shein walked in.

Don't ask me what we talked about all morning. I didn't hear a word.

I was thinking hard, thinking about Sean and Arjun. What was I going to tell them tomorrow when they asked to see the werewolf photos?

Would I have to confess that I'd lied to them?

No, I decided. I had a better plan.

"I'm going to sneak out tonight and take pictures of the Marlings' house," I whispered into the phone.

"Huh? Alex? Why are you whispering?" Hannah's voice rang shrilly in my ear.

I was whispering because my aunt and uncle had only one telephone. An old-fashioned black phone set on a table in the living-room. And the two of them were in the next room preparing dinner. I could see them from the armchair I was slumped in.

"Hannah, I'm going to hide at the side of the house," I whispered. "And I'm going to snap some pictures of whoever—or whatever—jumps out of that bedroom window tonight."

"Do you have a sore throat or something?" Hannah demanded. "I can't hear you, Alex."

I opened my mouth to repeat what I'd said—but Aunt Marta entered the room. "Dinner is ready, Alex. Who are you talking to?" she asked.

"Hannah," I told my aunt. "I've got to go," I

said into the phone. "Talk to you later." I hung up the receiver.

I hoped that Hannah might want to sneak out at midnight and keep me company. I'll have to ask her later, I decided.

Yawning, pretending to be very sleepy, I went to my room a little after ten o'clock. A few minutes later, I heard the lock click outside my door. My aunt or uncle had locked me in again.

But this time, I'd fooled them. This time, I was prepared.

Before dinner, I'd jammed a wad of bubble gum into the latch. The door wasn't really closed.

Once again, I pulled on an extra sweater. And checked my camera. And waited, gazing at the bedside clock.

Just before midnight, I swung the camera case over my shoulder. Slid the bedroom door open easily. And crept out of the house, under the white light of the moon, ready to solve the mystery of the Marlings.

I cast a quick glance at the Marlings' house. Then I turned away and trotted across the wet grass to Hannah's house.

No lights were on. The storm door at the back hadn't been shut. The wind made it swing open, as if inviting me in.

But I made my way up to Hannah's bedroom window on the other side of the house. Silver moonlight washed over the glass, making it reflect the trees like a mirror.

I couldn't see inside. But the window was open a few centimetres.

"Hannah—?" I called in a loud whisper. "Hannah—are you awake?"

I heard someone stirring inside. The curtains shifted. "Who's there?" Hannah called out sleepily.

"It's me!" I whispered, standing on tiptoe. "It's Alex. Come to the window."

"Alex? What are you doing out there?" she demanded.

"I'm going to take photos of the Marlings," I told her. "Come out with me, Hannah."

"Huh? Photos?" she called out. "But it's so late, Alex. I was asleep, and—"

"Every night I hear howls from their house," I told her. "And then someone—or something—jumps out of their bedroom window and runs into the woods. My uncle says it's their dogs, but—"

"I've told you," she interrupted. "The Marlings don't have dogs. They're werewolves. I know you don't believe me. But it's true. Your aunt and uncle know it's true. But they don't want you to be scared."

"That's why I want to take photos," I explained. "I mean, I could be the first person in the *world* to get a werewolf on film! Get dressed, Hannah. Come on!" I pleaded. "I want you to see too."

"You're crazy, Alex! Get back in the house!" Hannah warned. She appeared at the window. She pulled it up higher and leant out.

"I'm not coming out there," she insisted. "It's too dangerous. You told me about those two animals you saw. They were ripped to shreds—right? If the Marlings see you, they'll do the same thing to you!"

Her words sent a cold shiver down the back

of my neck. But I was desperate to solve the mystery—and to snap a great photo.

"They won't see us!" I told her. "We'll hide behind the bushes at the side of the house."

"Don't say *us*," Hannah called out. "I'm not doing it, Alex. I'm too scared. I'm warning you, go back inside."

"Please!" I pleaded. I grabbed her arm. "Come on out, Hannah. You want to see the werewolves too—don't you?"

"No way!" She jerked her arm away. "Go home, Alex," she repeated. "It's not a game. It's really dangerous."

"Listen, Hannah—" I started.

But she slid the window shut.

I stared at the reflection of the trees in the glass. Maybe she's right, I thought. Another cold shiver ran down my back. Maybe this is a big mistake. Maybe it *is* too dangerous. If the Marlings catch me . . .

I gasped when I heard a low growl.

I froze.

I didn't have to turn round. I knew from the sound.

A werewolf—it had sneaked up behind me.

Another low grunt made me cry out.

My knees started to collapse. I took a deep, shivering breath and spun round to face the creature.

No.

Not there.

No one there.

I swallowed. Swallowed again. My mouth suddenly felt bone-dry.

Another growl. I realized where it came from. From the back of the Marlings' house.

They're about to jump out of the window, I told myself. Those are the sounds I hear every night just before they climb out of the bedroom window.

And I'm standing out here in the open. I'll be the first thing they see!

My legs didn't want to work. But I gritted my teeth, took a deep breath—and forced myself to move.

My trainers slid on the wet grass. I slipped, but I didn't fall.

I scrambled to the bushes that divided my aunt and uncle's house from the Marlings' house.

I dropped to my knees, panting noisily. My heart pounded so hard, my chest hurt.

I ducked my head. And grabbed for the straps on my camera case.

A high, shrill animal howl floated out from the Marlings' open bedroom window. The light of the moon made the side of their house gleam.

The yard was nearly as bright as day. Everything glistened from the frosty dew.

Ducking low behind the bushes, I could see every leaf, every dew-covered blade of grass.

I tugged at the zip of my camera case. I knew I had to pull the camera out—quickly. But my hands were shaking so badly, I couldn't budge the zip.

Another howl made me turn back to the window.

A shadow moved.

A leg slid out.

Another leg.

A slender form dropped to the ground.

It all happened so quickly. As if time had been put on fast-forward.

My eyes on the window, I struggled to unzip the camera case.

Another body crawled out from the darkness of the Marlings' bedroom window.

Two forms stood on the ground and stretched.

Two *humans*!

Not wolves.

Humans.

What were they wearing?

Capes?

Dark fur capes, draped over their shoulders, hanging heavily behind them.

They had their backs to me. I couldn't see their faces.

Hands on their waists, they stretched, bending back, bending from side to side, as if limbering up their muscles for a long jog.

And then they raised their heads to the moon—and howled.

Turn round! I pleaded silently, trembling behind the bushes. *Please turn round! I want to see your faces!*

"Ohhhh . . ." I uttered a startled moan as their fur capes began to move. The heavy capes began to curl round them, to tighten around their bodies.

And I realized they weren't capes. They were some kind of animal skins.

Furry skins. With arms. And legs . . .

The dark skins wrapped themselves tightly over the two humans. The fur spread over their bodies, slid over their heads, covered their legs, their arms, their hands.

"Ohhhhh . . ." I shook so hard, I let go of the camera case and hugged myself. Hugged myself tightly, trying to hold myself in, trying to keep myself together.

The two figures howled again, raising their furry arms over their heads. Silvery claws slid out from their paws.

The two creatures raked the claws at each other playfully, pretending to attack. Growling and grunting, they lowered themselves to all fours.

No longer humans.

Animals . . . wolf creatures . . .

Hannah is right, I realized. She had told the truth. The Marlings *are* werewolves. They had turned into wolves under the moonlight.

Gasping for breath, I snatched up the camera case. I fumbled once again with the zip. Finally managed to pull it open.

And they turned. They both burned towards me.

Two *wolves*!

Their dark eyes stared out from beneath fur-covered foreheads. Their furry snouts snapped open to reveal rows of curled animal teeth.

Werewolves. The Marlings were werewolves. Human and wolf at the same time!

The werewolves nuzzled each other, growling softly. I raised the camera. I pulled myself up to my knees.

I've got to snap a picture. Do it *now*, Alex! I ordered myself.

But my hands shook so badly, I wasn't sure I could hold the camera steady enough.

Do it! Do it!

I raised the viewfinder to my eye. I stood up a little higher to see over the top of the bush.

"Ohhh." As I raised myself, a sharp twig scraped the side of my face.

And I dropped the camera!

It landed on the grass with a *THUD*.

The two wolf creatures turned.

And saw me!

I sank to the ground. Pressed myself flat on my stomach.

My chest heaved. I breathed through my mouth, struggling to keep perfectly still, perfectly silent.

Had they seen me? *Had* they?

I raised my head enough to peer out at them beneath the bottom branch of the bush.

They had their fur-covered snouts raised. They sniffed the air.

Could they *smell* me? Did they know I was hiding down here?

Were they about to leap into the bush and rip me apart with those long, silvery claws?

I held my breath, squinting across the grass at them.

They sniffed again, grunting softly.

Then they turned away. Dropped to all fours. And loped off, heading for the woods.

I waited until I could no longer hear the soft

thud of their paws or their low growls and grunts. Then I slid forward on my stomach, reached out, and grabbed my camera.

My camera!

I hadn't snapped any photos. Not a single shot.

I climbed shakily to my feet and rubbed the wet dew from the lens. Then I raised my eyes to the woods.

I have to follow them, I decided.

I have to take some photos. This is the chance of a lifetime!

If I can take the first-ever shots of actual werewolves, I'll be famous! I pictured myself in newspapers and on magazine covers. I imagined my photos of the Marlings on display in fancy photo galleries.

And I thought of how proud of me Uncle Colin and Aunt Marta would be.

That thought send a chill down my back. Uncle Colin and Aunt Marta—they were working in the woods right now. Busy photographing animals of the night.

Did they know that two werewolves were on the loose? Did they know that two werewolves were prowling the woods, searching for victims?

They're not safe out there, I realized.

Of course, following the werewolves into the woods was crazy—and dangerous. But now I had *two* reasons to chase after them.

I had to snap some pictures—*and* warn my aunt and uncle.

My eyes on the woods, I jammed the camera into the case and slung it over my shoulder. Then I began trotting across the back garden towards the trees, following the fresh paw prints in the frosty grass.

I ducked into the trees and followed the curving path. Moonlight trickled through the treetop leaves, making eerie, shifting patterns on the ground.

I didn't have to go far to catch up with the two werewolves. Just past the bent, old-man tree, I heard an animal grunt. And then a shrill cry of attack.

I stopped—and peered through a low evergreen shrub. Mouths gaping open, claws raised, the two wolf-creatures leapt.

They've caught someone! I realized, frozen in horror.

Who is it? My aunt? My uncle?

The two werewolves wrestled with their prey.

I heard a shrill bleat of pain. Then I saw four hooves shoot up in the air.

Not a human, I realized, squinting into the dim light. They've trapped a deer. A baby deer.

They're going to kill it.

They're going to tear it to shreds.

What can I do? I asked myself. How can I save it?

I didn't think. I was too terrified to think clearly.

I threw back my head. And I let out a loud wolf howl.

My cry echoed off the trees.

The snarling werewolves stopped their attack. They raised their heads.

They turned towards my cry.

Just long enough for the fawn to scramble to its feet. It shook itself—like a dog after a bath— and took off into the trees.

The werewolves sniffed the air furiously. They didn't seem to notice that the fawn had escaped.

Their eyes glowed red in the pale moonlight.

They turned, uttering low, angry growls.

Lowered their heads.

And came charging at me.

I staggered back.

Too frightened to move.

No time to run.

The ground seemed to shake under the thunder of the wolves' paws.

I opened my mouth to scream—but no sound came out.

The wolves' jaws snapped. Their red eyes glowed as if on fire.

I raised my arms in front of me, as if to shield myself.

Prepared for the attack.

And the wolves turned away. Turned sharply to the right, running together.

A scrawny brown rabbit scrambled over the path.

The wolves had turned away from me to chase the rabbit!

Snarling furiously, they lowered their heads—and caught the rabbit easily.

95

The little creature didn't put up much of a fight.

One wolf snapped its neck. The other bit hungrily into its belly.

Breathing hard, I swung my camera case round. And pulled the camera out with a quick jerk.

My hand trembled as I raised the viewfinder to my eye. But I steadied the camera with both hands.

And clicked off a shot.

And then another.

I snapped a shot of the wolves tugging the rabbit apart. And another shot of the two of them eating side by side.

When the wolves had finished, nothing remained of the rabbit. Licking their teeth, they turned and loped off into the trees.

Holding my camera in front of me with both hands, I followed them.

I suppose I was in some kind of shock. I know I wasn't thinking clearly.

I was barely thinking at all!

I had nearly been caught by the two were-wolves. They would have finished me the way they'd finished that poor rabbit.

But I knew I had to follow them. I had to stay in the woods.

I had to warn my aunt and uncle. I had to find them and tell them they were wrong about the Marlings. That Hannah had told the truth.

I had to let them know the danger they were in.

And I had to take more photographs.

I'd been through such a horrible scare. My heart pounded and my arms and legs felt all trembly and weak. I didn't feel like me. I felt as if I were outside myself, watching myself.

But I knew I couldn't run back to the house. Not until my aunt and uncle were safe.

I kept pretty far behind the creatures, far enough that I could slip behind a tree or bush if one of them glanced back. And I kept my camera raised, ready to snap off shots.

They loped slowly to the creek. I watched them lower their heads and noisily lap up water.

They didn't look at all human now. Their bodies had become wolf bodies. I couldn't see anything human in their faces. Their glowing eyes were animal eyes.

They took a long drink from the creek, washing down their dinner, I suppose. I steadied my camera and clicked off several shots.

I wished Hannah had come with me. I wanted someone else to be there with me, to see what I was seeing.

I couldn't wait to get back and tell her that she was right about the Marlings. That they really were werewolves.

The two wolf creatures suddenly raised their heads from the water, turned and sniffed the air.

Could they smell me? Or some other prey?

I slid behind a fat tree trunk and held my breath.

When I carefully peered out, they were loping along the creek shore. I waited until they had gone a short distance, then I crept out and followed them.

I followed the two werewolves all night. I finished one roll of film, then popped in another. I shot them rising up on their furry hind legs and howling at the moon. And I clicked off several more horrifying shots of them devouring small animals.

And I searched for my aunt and uncle. Desperate to warn them, to tell them what I had learned.

As I trailed behind the creatures—so frightened and excited—I completely lost track of time. It was as if I were walking through a dream. None of it seemed real.

Finally, a red crack of sunlight appeared along the ground. To my shock, it was nearly daybreak.

The werewolves moved slowly now. Their loping trot had become a stiff-legged walk.

As they stepped out of the trees into their back garden, they rose up on to their hind legs.

They staggered awkwardly to the back of their house.

I stayed by the trees, afraid to go too close. The sky was brightening as the sun made its way higher. If the wolf creatures turned round, they could see me easily.

I raised my camera. I had only a few shots left.

The two werewolves staggered on two legs to the side of their house. They stretched their furry forearms and raised their faces to the brightening sun.

"Oh!" I couldn't help it. I uttered a shocked cry as they began to shed their skins.

The fur appeared to peel back.

The claws slid out of view. And the fur pulled back, revealing their human hands.

As I gaped in amazement, the black wolf fur peeled off their arms and legs, then slid off their bodies.

They had their backs to me.

The fur skins settled into capes again. The two humans reached up and pulled off the heavy capes.

I'm going to see the Marlings for the first time! I realized.

They lowered the wolfskin capes to the ground.

They turned slowly.

And I saw their faces.

As the morning sunlight washed over their faces, I nearly cried out—in horror and disbelief.

Uncle Colin and Aunt Marta stretched, brushed back their silvery hair, then bent to pick up their wolfskins.

My aunt and uncle—*they were the werewolves!*

Uncle Colin raised his eyes to the woods. I fell back behind a tree. Had he seen me?

No.

My whole body trembled. I wanted to cry out: "No! No! This can't be happening!"

But I pressed myself against the tree and kept my jaws clamped tight. I couldn't let them see me. I couldn't let them know that I knew the truth.

The smooth tree trunk felt cool against my forehead. I had to think. I had to make a plan.

What should I do? I knew I couldn't stay with them any longer. I couldn't live in a house with two werewolves.

But where could I go? Who would help me? Who would *believe* me?

I watched my aunt and uncle fold up their wolfskins. Then Uncle Colin helped Aunt Marta climb into the Marlings' bedroom window. Once she was inside, he followed her in.

"The Marlings!" I murmured to myself. Were they okay in there? Or had my aunt and uncle done something terrible to them?

A few minutes later, Uncle Colin and Aunt Marta climbed back out of the window. Then they scurried across the driveway, into their own house.

I clung to the tree trunk for a while, watching the two houses. Thinking hard.

Were the Marlings asleep in their house? Did they know that the two werewolf skins were in there? Were the Marlings werewolves too?

I wanted to run away. To make my way to the street and just keep running until I was miles and miles away.

But I had to find out about the Marlings. I couldn't leave without finding out the truth about them.

So I watched the two houses for a while longer. No sign of anyone moving about.

I pushed myself away from the tree and quickly made my way through the Marlings' overgrown garden.

I ducked behind bushes and kept my eyes on my aunt and uncle's house. The blinds on their bedroom windows were shut.

Holding my breath, I darted to the Marlings' bedroom window. I grabbed the window-sill and peered inside. Dark. I couldn't see anything.

"Here goes," I murmured softly. "Good luck, Alex."

I lifted myself up on to the sill, then lowered my legs into the room. It took a few seconds for my eyes to adjust to the dim light.

And then what I saw shocked me nearly as much as learning that my aunt and uncle were werewolves.

I saw *nothing*.

The bedroom was completely bare. Not a stick of furniture. No artwork or mirrors on the wall. No carpet over the dust-covered floor-boards.

Turning to the bedroom door, I spotted the two wolfskins. They were neatly folded and piled side by side in front of the wardrobe.

Taking a deep breath, I moved cautiously to the open doorway. I poked my head out into the hall. Also unlit and bare.

"Anyone home?" I choked out in a tiny voice. "Hello? Anyone home?"

Silence.

I crept down the hall towards the front of the house. I peered into each room.

They were all bare and empty, covered with a thick layer of dust.

I stepped into the middle of the living-room. No furniture. No lights. No sign that anyone had lived there in years!

"Oh, wow!" I cried out as I realized the truth. My voice echoed off the bare walls.

No one lives here, I told myself. There *are* no Marlings!

My aunt and uncle had made them up. They used this house to hide their wolfskins. They'd made up the Marlings to keep people out of the house.

No Marlings. No Marlings. No Marlings.

It was all a lie!

I have to warn Hannah, I decided. No one is safe round here.

I pictured my aunt and uncle devouring that helpless little rabbit last night. I pictured them wrestling with that baby deer.

I have to tell Hannah and her family, I decided. And then we have to run away from here—as far as we can.

I turned and made my way quickly through the empty house. Then I lowered myself out of the bedroom window into the garden.

The morning sun was still a red ball, low over

the treetops. The early dew glistened over the grass.

"Hannah, I hope you're awake," I murmured. "If not, I'll have to wake you up."

I turned away from the Marlings' window and began to run across the back towards Hannah's house.

I went about six or seven steps. Then I stopped with a gasp as Aunt Marta's voice rang out behind me. *"Alex—what on earth are you doing out there?"*

I spun round. My knees nearly collapsed. The ground tilted up, then down.

Aunt Marta stood in the kitchen doorway. "Alex—why are you up so early? It's Saturday morning." She narrowed her eyes at me suspiciously.

"I—well . . ." I was shaking so hard, I couldn't speak!

"Where are you going in such a hurry?" my aunt demanded. I saw Uncle Colin standing behind her in the kitchen.

"To . . . Hannah's," I managed to reply. "To talk about . . . uh . . . our costumes for trick-or-treating tonight."

I watched her face. Did she believe me?

I didn't think so.

"It's too early to be running over to Hannah's," she scolded. She motioned for me to come inside. "Come in, Alex. Have some breakfast first."

I hesitated. My mind whirred.

Should I make a run for it? Run to the street and keep going?

How far would I get before they caught me? My aunt and uncle were both werewolves. If they caught me—what would they do to me? Would I be their breakfast?

No. I decided not to run. Not just yet, anyway. Not until I had a chance to talk to Hannah.

I felt Aunt Marta's eyes on me as I made my way slowly into the house. Uncle Colin muttered good morning. He stared hard at me too. "Early start, huh?" he asked softly.

I nodded and took my place at the breakfast table.

"Marta and I worked all night," Uncle Colin reported. He yawned. "We took some pretty good shots."

That's a lie! I wanted to shout. *I followed you. I saw what you did. I know what you are!*

But I didn't say anything. Just stared down at my cereal bowl.

I'm having breakfast with two werewolves! I thought, feeling my stomach churn. My aunt and uncle run through the woods at night, murdering and ripping animals apart.

I can't sit here another minute! I told myself. I started to get up.

But I felt Uncle Colin's hand on my shoulder. "Relax, Alex. Have a nice breakfast," he said softly.

"But, I—" I didn't know what to say. I was too terrified to eat. I wanted him to take his hand off me. It was making my whole body tremble.

"It's Hallowe'en," Uncle Colin said. "You'll be out late tonight."

"Have a good breakfast," Aunt Marta chimed in.

They watched me as I choked down my corn flakes. They were studying me coldly.

They know that I followed them, I decided. They know that I know their secret.

They're not going to let me get away.

"Uh . . . I have to go to Hannah's now," I said, struggling to sound calm and cheerful. I slid my chair back and started to stand up.

But I felt Uncle Colin's hand grip my shoulder again. He grasped me tightly and held on.

"Alex, come with me," he ordered.

He kept his hand clamped tightly on my shoulder as he led me to the back of the garage. He walked quickly and didn't say a word.

I wondered if I could break out of his grip and make a run for it. How far would I get?

He let go of my shoulder. What did he plan to do?

"I'm sorry I followed you," I said in a choked whisper. "I—I won't tell anyone what I saw."

He hadn't heard me. He had moved to the corner of the garage and picked up a long-handled tool.

He shoved it towards me. "I need your help this morning," he said. "There's a lot of gardening to be done."

I swallowed. "Gardening?"

Uncle Colin nodded. "That's a weed whacker. Have you ever used one before?"

"No. Not really," I confessed. The handle shook in my hand.

"It's pretty easy," he said. "I need you to cut down all these weeds behind the garage."

"Yeah. Okay," I replied, feeling dazed.

"And be careful not to throw any weeds into the Marlings' garden," he warned. "I'm sure they'll be watching your every move. Waiting to complain to us about you."

"No problem," I replied.

There are no Marlings! I wanted to scream.

"I'll work with you," Uncle Colin said, wiping sweat off his forehead with the back of his hand. "Together we can teach these weeds a lesson they'll never forget." He grinned for the first time that morning.

Does he know that I know? I wondered. Is that why he's keeping me here this morning?

My uncle and I worked in the garden all day. Whenever I took a short break, I'd catch him watching me coldly, studying me.

I was so frightened. I wanted to drop my tools and run.

But I couldn't leave without warning Hannah and her family. They had to know that they were in danger too.

I didn't see Hannah until after dinner. She burst in just as we were finishing.

"Well? How do I look?" she demanded. She did a fast twirl in her rag-doll costume.

"You look wonderful!" Aunt Marta gushed.

Hannah frowned at me. "Alex, where's your costume? Come on. You're not ready to trick-or-treat?"

"Uh . . . it's upstairs," I told her. "It won't take me long to get it together. Uh . . . come and help me—okay?"

I practically pulled her all the way to my room.

"It's a great night out," she said. "Perfect for trick-or-treating. The night of the full moon."

I tugged her into the room and shut the door behind us. "We've got a problem," I told her.

She fiddled with the rag hat that flopped down over her forehead. "Problem?"

"Yeah. Uncle Colin and Aunt Marta are werewolves."

"Huh?" Her eyes bulged. "What did you say?"

I explained everything. Speaking rapidly in a low whisper, I told her all that I'd seen last night. "They hide their wolfskins in the Marlings' house," I finished.

"But the Marlings—?" Hannah started.

"There *are* no Marlings!" I cried. "The house is empty. My aunt and uncle use it as a hiding-place for their wolfskins."

Hannah stared at me open-mouthed for a long time. Her chin trembled. "But . . . what are we going to *do*?" she cried breathlessly. "Your aunt and uncle—they seem like such nice people. They've always been so nice to me."

"They're werewolves!" I cried. "We have to tell your family. We have to hurry away from here. We have to get help. Tell the police or something."

"But—but—" Hannah sputtered, her face twisted in panic.

And suddenly I had another idea. "Wait!" I cried. "Hannah, what did Mr Shein say about werewolves shedding their skin? Didn't he say that if someone finds their skins and burns them, the werewolves will be destroyed?"

Hannah nodded. "Yes. That's what he said. But—"

"So that's what we'll do!" I cried excitedly. "We'll go next door, and—"

"But you don't want to *kill* your aunt and uncle—do you?" Hannah replied.

"Oh. No. Of course not," I told her. "I'm so frightened, I'm not thinking clearly. I just thought—"

"Whoa. Wait a minute, Alex!" Hannah cried, grabbing my arm. "I know what we can do. I have a plan that might work!"

I heard my aunt and uncle moving round in the living-room. Outside the bedroom window, the white full moon was rising behind the trees. Wisps of black cloud floated over it like wriggling snakes.

Hannah tugged me further into the room. "What if we *hide* the wolfskins?" she asked in an excited whisper.

"Hide them?" I whispered back. "What will that do?"

"Your aunt and uncle won't be able to find them," Hannah replied. "The night will pass. They won't be able to change into wolves."

"So maybe if they go a whole night without the skins, it will *cure* them!" I cried.

Hannah nodded. "It's worth a try, Alex. It might just work, and—" She stopped. "No. Wait. I have an even better idea. We'll *wear* the skins!"

"Excuse me?" I gasped. "Wear them? Why?"

"Because your aunt and uncle will search

everywhere for the skins," Hannah replied. "They'll search every house, every garage, every garden. But they won't look for them on us! That's the *last* place they'd look!"

"I get it," I replied. "And we'll make sure we stay away so they don't see us until after daybreak."

I wasn't sure whether the plan made any sense or not. Hannah and I were both too frightened to think!

Maybe . . . just maybe . . . we *could* cure Uncle Colin and Aunt Marta by keeping the skins from them until morning.

"Let's try it," I said.

"Okay," Hannah agreed. "Quick—get into your pirate costume. We don't want your aunt and uncle to suspect anything. While you're doing that, I'll sneak next door and slip on one of the wolfskins."

She pushed me towards the old clothes I had thrown on to the bed. "Hurry. It's getting late. Meet me at the back of the garage. I'll bring out your wolfskin for you."

Hannah disappeared out of the door. I heard her in the living-room. She said goodbye to Uncle Colin and Aunt Marta and told them she was going to meet me outside.

I heard the front door slam. Hannah was on her way next door to get the wolfskins.

I quickly pulled on the ragged old shirt and

113

torn trousers of my costume. I wrapped a bandanna around my head.

A sound at the bedroom door made me spin round.

"Aunt Marta!" I cried.

She stood in the doorway, frowning at me. "It won't work," she said, shaking her head.

"Huh?" I gasped.

"Alex, it won't work," she repeated unhappily.

My aunt moved quickly into the room.

I couldn't move. No time to try an escape.

"It won't work. That costume won't work," Aunt Marta said, shaking her head. "You need some make-up. Some black stains on your face. Something to make you look less clean!"

I burst out laughing. I had thought Aunt Marta had overheard our plan. But she only wanted to improve my pirate costume!

It took several minutes for my aunt to apply the make-up. Then she searched several drawers until she found a gold hoop earring, which she clipped on one ear.

"There. Much better," she said, grinning. "Now, hurry. Hannah is waiting for you."

I thanked her and hurried out. Hannah *was* waiting for me. Behind the garage. Already in a wolfskin.

I gasped when I saw her. It was so strange

seeing Hannah's eyes peering out from above a fur-covered snout.

"What took you so long?" she demanded. Her voice was muffled inside the furry wolf head.

"Aunt Marta," I replied. "She had to fix up my costume." I narrowed my eyes at Hannah. "How does it feel in there?"

"Very itchy," she grumbled. "And hot. Here." She handed me the other wolfskin. "Hurry. Put it on. The moon is already high. Your aunt and uncle will be looking for these soon."

I took the skin from her. My hand sank into the thick fur. I unfolded it and held it up. "Here goes," I whispered. "I *said* I wanted to be a werewolf for Hallowe'en. I suppose I get my wish."

"Just hurry!" Hannah urged. "We don't want them to catch us."

I pulled the wolfskin over my head. Down over the old clothes of my costume. It felt a little tight. Especially the furry legs. The face fitted snugly over my face.

"You're right. It's itchy," I groaned. "It's so tight. I'm not sure I can walk!"

"It loosens up after a bit," Hannah whispered. "Come on. Let's get away from here."

She led the way across the garden. Then we turned and trotted along the side of her house and down to the street.

I heard voices in the next block. Kids shouting, "Trick-or-treat!"

"We might be safer with other kids," I suggested. "I mean, if we find a whole group and stick with it . . ."

"Good idea," Hannah replied. We crossed the street.

It was already getting really hot inside my wolfskin. I could feel the sweat running down my forehead.

We walked for several blocks. But most of the kids were younger than us. We didn't find anyone good to hang out with.

We turned the corner and walked several more blocks, into the next neighbourhood.

"Hey—look who's there!" Hannah declared, bumping my arm.

I followed her gaze and saw a mummy and a robot carrying trick-or-treat bags across someone's front lawn.

"It's Sean and Arjun," Hannah cried.

"Let's trick-or-treat with them!" I suggested. I began running across the grass, waving my paw at them. "Hey, guys! Hey!"

They turned and stared at us.

"Wait up!" I called through my fur-covered snout.

They screamed. And dropped their bags. And took off, running full speed, shrieking for help.

Hannah and I stopped at the edge of a driveway and watched them run. "Think maybe we scared them?" Hannah said, laughing.

"Maybe a little," I replied.

We both laughed.

But not for long.

I heard heavy, running footsteps on the pavement behind us.

I turned—and let out a gasp as my aunt and uncle came running furiously down the street.

"There they are!" Uncle Colin cried, pointing at us. "*Get* them!"

31

I froze for a moment, horrified by the sight of my aunt and uncle running towards us so furiously, so desperately.

"Don't move!" Aunt Marta pleaded. "We need those skins!"

My legs refused to budge. But then Hannah gave me a hard shove. And we both took off.

We ran wildly, across lawns and empty plots. We cut behind someone's house, then dived through an opening in their tall hedge.

My aunt and uncle stayed close behind, running at full speed, and calling out as they ran, "Give us our skins! Give us our skins!"

Their breathless voices rang in my ears. Their words became an eerie chant.

"Give us our skins! Give us our skins!"

We must have run for blocks. It all became a dark blur to me. My heavy wolf paws thumped the ground. I struggled to keep my balance.

Sweat poured down my face inside the heavy fur.

Another turn. More dark back gardens. And then the tilting, tangled trees of the woods rose up in front of us.

Hannah and I dived into the woods, darting between the trees and tall weeds. And still my aunt and uncle came after us, chanting, chanting their desperate plea:

"Give us our skins! Give us our skins!"

We scrambled up a low hill lined with evergreens. Pine cones slid under my heavy paws and rolled down the hill. Hannah stumbled and dropped to her knees. She scrambled on all fours to the top.

"Give us our skins! Give us our skins!"

The cry grew shrill and breathless.

And then—suddenly—everything seemed to stop.

As if the whole world had stopped spinning.

As if even the wind had stopped blowing on top of that little hill.

I could *feel* the silence.

Uncle Colin and Aunt Marta had stopped their chant.

Panting, Hannah and I turned to face them.

"The moon—" Hannah whispered breathlessly to me. She pointed. "The full moon, Alex. It's so high. It must be at its peak."

And as she whispered those words, my aunt

and uncle dropped to their knees. They threw back their heads. As the white light of the moon washed over their faces, I saw their pain, their horror.

They opened their mouths in long, mournful howls.

Their howls became hideous screams. They tore at their hair with both hands. Shut their eyes. And screamed, screamed in agony.

"Hannah—what have we done?" I cried.

Tugging at their hair, my aunt and uncle screamed.

And then, they lowered their hands. And closed their mouths. And a calm seemed to sweep over them.

As Hannah and I stared down at them, Uncle Colin and Aunt Marta helped each other to their feet. They brushed each other off. Smoothed down their hair.

When they finally gazed up at us, I saw tears in their eyes.

"Thank you," they both cried.

"Thank you for saving us!" Uncle Colin exclaimed.

And then they rushed up the hill to hug us, hug us so joyfully.

"You freed us from the curse!" Aunt Marta declared, tears running down her face. "The moon reached the highest point in the sky and we didn't transform. Colin and I are no longer werewolves!"

"How can we ever thank you?" Uncle Colin cried. "You are both so wonderful. So brave."

"So *hot*!" I grumbled. "I can't wait to get out of this itchy skin!"

Everyone laughed.

"Let's go back to our house!" Aunt Marta cried. "We'll have a real celebration!"

The four of us hurried back to the house. We laughed and joked all the way.

Uncle Colin and Aunt Marta made their way in through the kitchen door. "Home-made doughnuts!" Aunt Marta promised. "And big mugs of hot chocolate! How does that sound?"

"Sounds great!" Hannah and I agreed.

Hannah started to follow them into the house. But I held her back.

"Let's dump the skins next door," I said. "No one will ever need them again. Let's dump them in the abandoned house."

She hesitated. She seemed afraid to go back into that dark, empty house.

But I went running over the Marlings' house. I couldn't wait to take off the hot, smelly wolf-skin.

I pulled myself on to the window-ledge, then lowered my legs through the open bedroom window. I stepped into the room. Pale moonlight washed over the bare floorboards.

Hannah dropped into the room behind me. "Alex—?" she called.

I started to tug off the heavy wolfskin.

But something near the wardrobe caught my eye.

I stopped and walked over to it.

A folded-up wolfskin lay on the floor against the wall.

"Huh?"

I let out a startled cry. And turned to Hannah. "How can there be a wolfskin in here?" I asked. "There were only two of them—right? You put one on, and you gave one to me."

Hannah stepped up beside me. Her eyes locked on mine. "I didn't wear the one from this house, Alex," she said softly. "I used my own. I just got it last night."

"Huh?" I cried. "I don't get it."

"You will," she whispered.

She knocked me to the floor with her heavy forepaws and sank her teeth into my chest.